For my inspirational
and amazing children
Mollie and William.

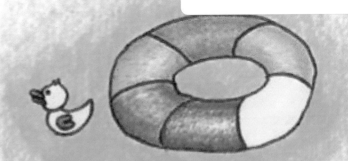

I would like to thank my husband, family and all my friends
for all their amazing help, support and encouragement.

ISBN 9798518873650

Text and illustration Copyright © Rebecca L Holmes 2021

Oh Dotty, don't be grotty!

Written and illustrated by Rebecca L Holmes

Dotty was feeling very grotty. She really wanted to play in the paddling pool but it was raining and Mum said that it was too cold.

Dotty felt **grotty!**

"Oh **Dotty**, don't be **grotty**!" Mum said.

"There are lots of other things that you can do!"

Dotty had an idea. "I know! I can play hide and seek with Lottie!"

Lottie was Dotty's favourite toy, but she was in the washing machine because she had got muddy when they played at the park.

Dotty felt **grotty!**

"Oh **Dotty**, don't be **grotty**!" Mum said.

"There are lots of other things that you can do!"

Dotty had another idea. "I know! I can bake some yummy cakes." But Dad was already cooking and there was no room in the kitchen.

Dotty felt **grotty!**

"Oh **Dotty**, don't be **grotty**!" Mum said.

"There are lots of other things that you can do!"

Dotty had an even better idea. "I know! I will find Deefa Dog and I can play with him." But Deefa Dog was asleep, and Dotty couldn't wake him.

Dotty felt **grotty**!

"Oh **Dotty**, don't be **grotty**!" Mum said.

"There are lots of other things that you can do!"

Dotty really was feeling very **grotty** and she didn't know what to do.

Then Mum shouted "Dotty, come and look!"

Dotty sighed a very big **grotty** sigh!

She slowly got up and went to find her Mum.

"Look outside, Dotty!"
Mum said, "the sun has
come out; and it's not
raining now!"

Dotty was so excited;
she ran to get her
inflatable ring and rubber
ducks.

Dotty was
not grotty
anymore!

Printed in Great Britain
by Amazon